波波的復活節

Justine Korman　著

Lucinda McQueen　繪

本局編輯部　譯

三民書局

For Ron, the grumpiest bunny of all
一J.K.

獻給朗，最愛嘀咕的兔寶寶
一J.K.

For Alex Guitar
一Lots of love from Aunt Lucy

獻給亞力克斯·吉塔
一 好多好多的愛，來自露西阿姨

Deep in the forest on the night
before **Easter**, the **bunnies** danced under the
moon. They were all as happy as...well, Easter
bunnies—except for one **grumpy** bunny named Hopper.

復活節前夕，在森林的深處，兔寶寶們在月光下跳著舞。他們全都好快樂，就像……
嗯，就像復活節兔寶寶一樣地開心——除了那隻愛抱怨、名叫波波的兔寶寶。

After the bunnies had finished dancing, Sir Byron, the Great Hare, told them, "You are the **messengers** of spring. Go now, and spread love and joy!"

Hopper kicked a stone and **grumbled**, "Joy and love. Ha! I hate that **mushy** stuff."

等兔寶寶們跳完了舞，兔老爹拜倫先生對大家說，「你們可都是春天的使者。現在，出發去散播愛與歡樂吧！」
波波踢著小石子嘀咕著，「歡樂和愛。哼！我討厭這種虛情假意的玩意兒。」

As he waited in line for his **wheelbarrow** full of Easter treats, Hopper grew even grumpier. What was the **point** of making treats all year and then running your paws off to hide them for someone else to find?

當波波排隊等待他那輛裝滿復活節小甜點的手推車時,他變得更不耐煩。真搞不懂,為什麼要花一整年的時間去做小甜點,然後再東奔西跑地把它們藏起來讓別人找呢?

當別的兔寶寶開始歡歡喜喜工作時，波波卻是慢吞吞地拖著早已疲憊的步伐。

While the other bunnies gladly began their rounds, Hopper dragged his already tired feet.

Hopper gazed at the heap of chocolate bunnies, **marshmallow** chicks, **caramels**, **raspberry** creams, and other delights.

"I wish all these treats were mine," he thought hungrily.

波波兩眼盯著整堆的兔寶寶巧克力、小雞糖、牛奶糖、樹莓奶油，以及其他可口的小點心。

「希望這些全都是我的，」他飢腸轆轆地想著。

Then his ears flew up with a **wicked** idea. "They *could* be mine!" he said. "Who will ever know if I keep the goodies or give them away?"

Hopper ran to his **burrow**, pushing the heavy wheelbarrow as fast as he could.

然後，他的耳朵豎了起來，他想到了一個壞主意。「它們可以變成我的呀！」他說。「誰會知道到底我是把糖果留了下來，還是發了出去呢？」

波波推起重重的推車，盡可能用最快的速度衝向他自己的洞穴。

Hopper tried to roll the heavy wheelbarrow inside, but it was too wide. He pushed and shoved and pushed some more. He was so busy pushing, Hopper didn't notice a strawberry-cream-filled egg fall off the wheelbarrow. The egg rolled down the **shady** path toward the stream.

波波試著把重重的推車推進去，可是推車太寬了，他推了又推，又再往前推一些。

波波忙著推啊推的，沒注意到一顆包著草莓奶油餡兒的蛋從推車上掉了下來。那顆蛋沿著陰暗的小徑，滾啊滾的滾到了小溪邊。

Hopper puffed up his tiny chest. Then he pushed **with all his might**. The wheelbarrow **lurched** forward, and the grumpy bunny **fell** flat **on his face**.

"That was almost as hard as delivering the treats," Hopper complained.

波波吸足一口氣，然後用盡全力一堆，手推車便歪歪斜斜地往前滑去，而他也跟著撲倒在地上。

「簡直就跟分送這些東西一樣困難嘛，」波波嘀咕著。

But at last, the goodies were inside. Hopper ran his paws through the mountain of candy. He **juggled** jellybeans and made marshmallow nests for the chocolate eggs.

可是最後，那些糖果終於在洞裡了。波波在像小山一樣高的糖果堆裡東跑跑西摸摸。他抓起QQ豆拋著玩，還用雪棉糖布置成巧克力蛋的巢。

Then he began to eat.

And eat.

And eat!

Hopper **gobbled** and **gnawed** the whole night through. Now he didn't feel so grumpy, but he did feel very sticky and a little too full.

接著，他就開始吃啊！吃啊！吃啊！

整個晚上，波波就一直狼吞虎嚥，大吃特吃。這個時候，他不再那麼愛抱怨了。可是他實在覺得很膩，而且太飽了點。

Finally, he decided to go to the stream to get a nice, cool drink. Hopper stopped when he heard a *mew, mew, mew*. He **peeked** out from behind a tree and saw Lottie, Spottie, and Dottie, three kittens who lived nearby.

最後，他決定到溪邊去喝點兒爽口清涼的水。
波波聽到一陣喵喵喵的叫聲，便停下了腳步。
他躲在樹後面偷看，看見了樂蒂、史帕蒂、朵蒂這三隻住在附近的小貓。

波波躲進蘆葦叢中偷聽。
「它們一定在某個地方，」史帕蒂說。

Hopper hid in the reeds and listened.
"They must be here somewhere," Spottie
mewed. "This is Easter morning, isn't it?" Lottie asked.
"Oh, dear," Hopper thought. "The kittens are searching for
Easter treats—and they aren't going to find any!"
Hopper felt an **uncomfortable stirring** deep inside. Should
he have eaten the treats? Had he done the wrong thing?

「現在是復活節的早晨，不是嗎？」樂蒂問。
「哦，天啊，」波波心想。「這些小貓在找復活節的小甜點──他們一定找不到的！」
波波感到很不安。他不該吃掉那些小甜點嗎？他做錯了嗎？

Then, to Hopper's great surprise, Dottie cried, "I found one!"
She had found the strawberry-cream-filled egg that had fallen off his wheelbarrow.

接著，令波波大吃了一驚的是，他聽見朵蒂叫著，「我找到一顆了！」
她找到從波波推車上掉下來的那顆包草莓奶油餡兒的蛋了。

Before Hopper could say a word, Spottie and Lottie rushed to their sister.

"I'm the oldest," Spottie said, grabbing for the egg.

"I'm the hungriest," Lottie argued.

"I found it!" Dottie **squeaked**.

波波還沒回過神來，史帕蒂跟樂蒂已經朝他們的小妹衝了過去。

「我年紀最大，」史帕蒂一邊說，一邊伸手去搶那顆蛋。

「我肚子最餓，」樂蒂吵著說。

「蛋是我找到的！」朵蒂拉高了嗓門叫著。

Hopper felt terrible as he watched the
kittens **wrestle** and **hiss** in the dewy grass.
    Suddenly, the kittens rolled right over the egg
and **smashed** it to bits. They stopped wrestling and
stared at the gooey mess.

看到小貓們在沾著露水的草地上扭打成一團，波波心裡愧咎極了。

忽然，小貓們滾到蛋上頭，把蛋壓成了碎片。他們不再扭打，直楞楞地望著那一團黏呼呼的東西。

"We should have shared," Spottie mewed sadly.

"We shouldn't have been **greedy**," Lottie sighed.

"We'll divide what's left of it," Dottie said firmly. Then the three kittens **hugged**.

「我們應該一起吃的，」史帕蒂傷心地喵喵叫。

「我們不該那麼貪心的，」樂蒂嘆了一口氣。

「我們把剩下的平分，」樂蒂堅定地說。接著，三隻小貓就抱在一起。

"Oh, dear," Hopper said to himself. He turned away from the kittens—only to find himself nose-to-nose with Sir Byron, the Great Hare!

"Why haven't you delivered to your area?" Sir Byron **demanded**.

Hopper opened his mouth, but no sound came out. The chocolate that was **smeared** all over his face said it all.

「哦，天哪，」波波自言自語。他轉身要躲開那些小貓──卻發現自己的鼻子與兔老爹拜倫先生的鼻子對了個正著！

「你為什麼沒把甜點送到你負責的地方呢？」拜倫先生質問他。

波波張開了嘴，說不出話來。糊在他臉上的巧克力說明了一切。

「跟我來，」拜倫先生說。

波波跟著他往洞穴走，小貓們緊跟在後。拜倫先生把波波吃剩的糖交給小貓們，並封他們為復活節兔寶寶的榮譽成員。

"Come with me," Sir Byron said.

Hopper followed him to the burrow, and the kittens **tagged** along behind. Sir Byron gave the kittens what was left of Hopper's goodies and made them honorary Easter bunnies.

"Go now," Sir Byron told the kittens. "Spread joy and love!"

The Great Hare turned to Hopper. "As for you," he said, "you shall watch the kittens hide your treats. Perhaps then you'll understand what it means to be an Easter bunny."

「現在，出發，」拜倫先生對小貓們說。「去散播歡樂與愛吧！」

兔老爹轉向波波。「至於你呢，」他說，「你得看著小貓們把你所負責的小甜點藏起來。也許這樣一來，你會了解身為復活節兔寶寶的意義。」

It took a while for the kittens to get the **knack** of hippety-hopping. But they had no trouble at all spreading joy.

Hopper followed as they crossed the forest, hiding a brightly colored egg here, a chocolate bunny there. He watched as young **gophers**, **squirrels**, **moles**, and mice squeaked with delight as they found their treats.

Hopper looked up and saw the clouds change from pink to **fluffy** white. He saw the first **crocuses** open their **petals**.

小貓們花了一點功夫學習跳躍的秘訣。但散播歡樂這回事對他們來說可就不成問題了。
波波跟著他們穿過森林，在這兒藏了個彩蛋，在那兒藏了個兔寶寶巧克力。

他看見小地鼠、松鼠、小鼬鼠、還有小老鼠都因為找到小點心而高興地吱吱叫。
波波抬頭看見雲朵從粉紅色變成毛茸茸的白色。他看到了第一朵番紅花的花瓣綻放了。

Hopper felt a lump in his throat. He'd always just worked his **route**, then gone home to **soak** his sore paws. He had never noticed the wonder and magic of Easter before. It made him feel happy inside.

Just then Sir Byron appeared at his side. "What do you think about Easter now, Hopper?"

"It's wonderful!" Hopper said.

波波感動到連喉嚨都哽住了。他一向只照著自己的路線工作，然後回家泡泡酸痛的腳。在這之前，他從沒注意過復活節的神奇與魔力。而現在，他所感受到的令他打從心底高興了起來。

這時候拜倫先生出現在他身旁。「現在，你對復活節有什麼看法呢，波波？」

「復活節真是美妙啊！」波波說。

From then on, Hopper was glad to be an Easter bunny. He didn't mind spending every day of the year making treats for others to enjoy.

And the next year, for the first time in his life, Hopper was eager for the night before Easter.

從此以後，波波便以身為復活節兔寶寶為樂。他不再介意花一整年的時間去做小點心給別人享用了。

第二年，是波波生平第一次期待著復活節前夕的到來。

Finally the magic night arrived. Hopper's feet felt
as **light** as marshmallow chicks as he danced the
Easter bunny dance. He couldn't wait to get his
wheelbarrow heaped with treats and hide them all
over the woods for happy **youngsters** to find.

終於，這奇妙的夜晚降臨了。跳復活節兔子舞時，波波的腳步輕盈得就像棉花小雞軟糖一樣。

他等不及要將他的手推車裝滿小點心，然後把它們藏到森林裡的各個地方，好讓快樂的小朋友們去尋找。

When Sir Byron gave Hopper his wheelbarrow, he said, "Since you have an **awfully** big route for one little bunny, I've **arranged** for you to have some helpers."

Hopper laughed as the three little kittens popped out from behind the Great Hare.

當拜倫先生將波波的手推車交給他的時候,他說,「你的路程對一隻小兔寶寶來說太遠了,所以我幫你安排了幾個幫手。」

看到三隻小貓從拜倫先生的背後蹦出來,波波笑了起來。

And as they pushed their **delicious** load through the **moonlit** forest with a *hippety, hoppety, mew, mew, mew,* Hopper realized just how much happiness Easter brings.

　　而當他們推著好吃的點心，伴隨蹦蹦蹦、喵喵喵的聲音，走過月光照耀的森林時，波波終於了解到復活節帶來了好多好多的歡樂。

30

demand [dɪˋmænd] 動 質問

 A

arrange [əˋrendʒ] 動 安排
awfully [ˋɔfʊlɪ] 副 非常地

 E

Easter [ˋistɚ] 名 復活節

 B

bunny [ˋbʌnɪ] 名 兔寶寶
burrow [ˋbɝo] 名 洞穴

 F

fall on one's face 面朝下跌倒
fluffy [ˋflʌfɪ] 形 毛茸茸的

 C

caramel [ˋkærəml̩] 名 牛奶糖
crocus [ˋkrokəs] 名 番紅花

 G

gnaw [nɔ] 動 嚙咬
gobble [ˋgɑbl̩] 動 狼吞虎嚥
gopher [ˋgofɚ] 名 地鼠
greedy [ˋgridɪ] 形 貪婪的
grumble [ˋgrʌmbl̩] 動 發牢騷
grumpy [ˋgrʌmpɪ] 形 愛抱怨的

 D

delicious [dɪˋlɪʃəs] 形 美味的

marshmallow [`marʃ,mælo] 名 雪棉糖

messenger [`mɛsņdʒɚ] 名 使者

mole [mol] 名 鼴鼠

moonlit [`mun,lɪt] 形 月光照耀的

mushy [`mʌʃɪ] 形 太過於多愁善感的

hiss [hɪs] 動 發出嘶嘶聲

hug [hʌg] 動 擁抱

juggle [`dʒʌgḷ] 動 拋球雜耍

knack [næk] 名 訣竅

light [laɪt] 形 輕的

lurch [lɝtʃ] 動 突然傾斜

peek [pik] 動 偷看

petal [`pɛtḷ] 名 花瓣

point [pɔɪnt] 名 目的

raspberry [`ræz,bɛrɪ] 名 樹莓

route [rut] 名 路線

shady [`ʃedɪ] 形 陰暗的

smash [smæʃ] 動 砸碎

smear [smɪr] 動 弄髒

soak [sok] 動 浸泡

squeak [skwik] 動 吱吱地叫

squirrel [`skwɝəl] 名 松鼠

stirring [`stɝɪŋ] 名 小騷動

youngster [`jʌŋstɚ] 名 幼小的動物

tag [tæg] 動 緊跟著……走

uncomfortable [ʌn`kʌmfɚtəbl̩] 形 不安的

wheelbarrow [`hwil͵bæro] 名 獨輪手推車

wicked [`wɪkɪd] 形 邪惡的

with all one's might 傾全力

wrestle [`rɛsl̩] 動 扭打，摔角

~ 看的繪本＋聽的繪本　童話小天地最能捉住孩子的心 ~

為孩子寫～彩色的夢

 兒童文學叢書

·童話小天地·

◉ **奇妙的紫貝殼**
簡 宛·文　朱美靜·圖

◉ **九重葛笑了**
陳 冷·文　吳佩蓁·圖

◉ **銀毛與斑斑**
李民安·文　廖健宏·圖

◉ **屋頂上的祕密**
劉靜娟·文　郝洛玟·圖

◉ **石頭不見了**
李民安·文　翱 子·圖

◉ **奇奇的磁鐵鞋**
林黛嫚·文　黃子瑄·圖

◉ **智慧市的糊塗市民**
劉靜娟·文　郜欣／倪靖·圖

◉ **丁伶郎**
潘人木·文
鄭凱軍／羅小紅·圖

嘟～請你醫起耳朵，它會帶焦焦甜甜的說故事時間就要開始囉！

國家圖書館出版品預行編目資料

波波的復活節 / Justine Korman著;Lucinda McQueen
繪;[三民書局]編輯部譯.－－初版一刷.－－臺北
市；三民，民90
　　面；公分－－(探索英文叢書.波波唸翻天系列;1)
中英對照
ISBN 957-14-3440-X　(平裝)
　1.英國語言－讀本

805.18　　　　　　　　　　　　　90003944

網路書店位址　http://www.sanmin.com.tw

© 　波波的復活節

著作人　Justine Korman
繪　圖　Lucinda McQueen
譯　者　三民書局編輯部
發行人　劉振強
著作財　三民書局股份有限公司
產權人　臺北市復興北路三八六號
發行所　三民書局股份有限公司
　　　　地址 / 臺北市復興北路三八六號
　　　　電話 / 二五〇〇六六〇〇
　　　　郵撥 / 〇〇〇九九九八——五號
印刷所　三民書局股份有限公司
門市部　復北店 / 臺北市復興北路三八六號
　　　　重南店 / 臺北市重慶南路一段六十一號
初版一刷　中華民國九十年四月
編　號　S 85589
定　價　新臺幣壹佰玖拾元
行政院新聞局登記證局版臺業字第〇二〇〇號